D1681083

Aunt Val
and the
Three Noses

Valerie Salenski

Copyright © 2017 by Valerie Salenski. 749534

ISBN: Softcover   978-1-5245-8245-6
       EBook   978-1-5245-8246-3

All rights reserved. No part of this book may
be reproduced or transmitted in any form or by
any means, electronic or mechanical, including
photocopying, recording, or by any information
storage and retrieval system, without permission
in writing from the copyright owner.

This is a work of fiction. Names, characters,
places and incidents either are the product of
the author's imagination or are used fictitiously,
and any resemblance to any actual persons,
living or dead, events, or locales is entirely
coincidental.

Print information available on the last page

Rev. date: 02/17/2017

To order additional copies of this book, contact:
Xlibris
1-888-795-4274
www.Xlibris.com
Orders@Xlibris.com

Eight little cousins were at Grandma and Grandpa's house. They were very excited because Uncle Max was coming home from the Navy. But they were also tired of waiting, so....

"Aunt Val! Aunt Val! Tell us a story PLEEESE!" the children begged as they climbed up on the sofa. "OK then, what story do you want?" she asked.

Theresa said: "The Three Billy Goats!"

Patrick said: "No! The Three Bears!"

George said: "No! The Three Pigs!"

Eddie said: "The Three Anythings."

Rusty said: "The Three Billy Goats.

Josh shouted: "Bears for me."

Joe agreed with Josh.

Baby Marye said "Goo-Goo".

Aunt Val said: "Okay, Okay! I will tell them all". And she did. Twice. And they said; "AGAIN, AGAIN!" Then Joe sneezed three times. And Aunt Val said:

"I could tell you about three sneezes and it would make you happy.

"Yes! Yes!" They all shouted! "Tell us about The Three Sneezes!"

"How about noses instead of sneezes?" asked Aunt Val. Everyone was okay with noses. Aunt Val began: "Once upon a time there were three noses."

All the children shouted "YAAAY!" Aunt Val said, "Now be quiet because I am making this up as I go and I have to think about it."

The children were quiet. Then Aunt Val began again: "Once upon a time there were three people with very big noses. There was Sneezee the Nose, Smella the Nose, and Snorty the Nose." "Sneezee was the eldest of the siblings. He could sneeze hard enough to blow houses down."

"Just like the three pigs," said George. "I bet Sneezee knows the three pigs." said Josh. "No," said Aunt Val. "They lived in a different town."

Does Sneezee use a lot of tissues?" asked Patrick. "I bet he owns the tissue factory", said Josh. "Let's move on" said Aunt Val.

"Smella was the next oldest and she could smell anything, even from far away. She liked flowers and perfume, especially gardenias."

She really liked flowers, especially Gardenias because of the beautiful smell.

"What's a Gardna?" asked Theresa. "A Gardenia is a beautiful flower" said Aunt Val. "Oh," Theresa said. "I like it best, too". Aunt Val continued:

"Snorty, who was the youngest, made a loud snorting sound that could be heard far away." "Does he keep everyone awake at night?" asked Joe. Aunt Val said "It's not too bad, everyone uses ear plugs and Snorty sleeps in the barn".

SNEEZEE

The time came for Sneezee to leave home and find a job. He decided to go to the big city and maybe get work at the King's castle. On his way up a big hill he heard screaming. He ran to the hilltop and saw a giant destroying a village.

The giant stomped on the houses and ate all the food he could find.

"Stop!" Sneezee yelled. The giant didn't listen. Sneezee sneezed a very big sneeze. It blew the giant into a forest where he got tangled in tree branches.

Sneezee and the villagers found the giant. He promised he would not be bad again, he was just hungry. "But you were also mean," Sneezee said. "You must be judged by the King." Sneezee said.

Sneezee and the villagers chopped the tree down and they went to the castle. Soldiers stopped them at the castle gate. "How did you get a giant into a tree?" they asked. Sneezee and the villagers told them what the giant did. The soldiers said, "follow us." They all went to see the King. Sneezee told the King what the giant did.

The giant told the King that he was just hungry. The King said the giant had to build new houses for the villagers. The King would give him food. Sneezee and the soldiers were sent to make sure the giant finished the job.

When they all got back to the castle, the soldiers and Sneezee told the King the giant did a good job. So the King asked the giant to be his bodyguard. After all, who would make a better body guard than a giant?

The giant happily agreed. The King asked Sneezee to be the Captain of the army because he could sneeze the King's enemies away. Sneezee was happy to get such a good job so soon.

SMELLA

Smella was also looking for a job and headed for the castle. While walking she noticed a giant building houses and some soldiers standing by. She even thought she saw her brother, Sneezee. As she walked, she stopped to pick many fragrant flowers. Then she began to smell something horrible!

She had to find out how she could get rid of it. So she followed her nose to a small house with a really bad smell. Smella knocked on the door and an old man opened it. "Who are you?" he asked. "My name is Smella the Nose, and I would like to help you get rid of the horrible smell that brought me here.

"Is it that bad?" he asked. "I am sorry to say it is" Smella said. "I just want to help you." The old man, whose name is Paul, told her he had been the King's perfume maker for many years, but now he can't smell at all. Smella said, "I can help you make beautiful scents if you will bury what you just made."

The old man was happy to have such a helper. He dug a hole and buried the smelly perfume. Smella showed Paul the flowers she had picked. They worked together to make a sweet perfume.

The next day, they went to the castle and sold it all. Paul said "let's go make some more!"

As they were leaving, Smella saw her brother, Sneezee, wearing armor and a helmet. Boy, was she surprised! She introduced him to Paul and told him about their perfume business. He told her about the giant and being made the Captain of the army. They both wondered what Snorty was doing.

SNORTY

Snorty was walking along the seashore. He saw a village close by and hoped to find a job. But a huge bank of fog filled the village, and the fishermen could not find their way home. Snorty ran to a dock, and snorted his loudest snort every minute. The fishermen followed the noise back to their own village.

When the fishermen got off their boats, they saw Snorty. "Did you hear a very loud noise?" asked one of the fishermen. "That was me" Snorty replied. "With a nose like mine, I can snort really loud." The fishermen all laughed and shook his hand to thank him. One man asked Snorty to stay with them for the night.

The next day, all of the fishermen asked Snorty to be their Mayor. Snorty was surprised. He said, "I don't know what a Mayor does". "We will find out," said a fisherman. So, Snorty and three fishermen went to see the King. When they got to the castle, the fishermen told the King how Snorty saved them.

They asked the King to make him their Mayor. The King agreed. Snorty asked what he had to do. The King said: collect taxes, solve problems and perform weddings. The King would pay his wages.

Then the King said "You look a lot like my Captain of the Guard, Sneezee, and his sister, Smella, the Royal Perfume Maker. "I am their brother!" He said.

The King called for a feast in honor of the whole Nose family including Mom the Nose and Dad the Nose. Everyone was proud of each other and promised to visit. Then they each went on their way sneezing, snorting and smelling wonderful.

Before Aunt Val could say THE END
the children were running to the door.

Uncle Max walked in. He was home.
Everyone was happy.

THE END FOR REAL